The
Christmas Shark

By

Shae Archambault…and her dad.

PROCEEDS

All proceeds will be donated to the Surfrider Foundation. By purchasing – The Christmas Shark – you have made a commitment to protecting our oceans. And we thank you.

Dedicated to Tate and Laurie

Illustrated by Marcelo Simonetti

Lightning was a huge great white shark who lived in the waters off
the Monterey coast. He was a very fast shark and always swam
alone. On this Christmas Eve day Lightning swam in from the
deep… looking…waiting.

First, he approached Point Lobos Cove.

"Shark! Shark!", yelped the otters as they quickly swam into their underwater cave to hide.

He then glided toward Sea Lion Point where the seals and sea lions jumped and played.

The elder sea lion, sensing something approaching, leapt to the
highest rock and barked, "Shark! Shark!" All the pups raced out

As evening approached people gathered in the seaside town of Carmel.

They celebrated with Christmas carols and hot chocolate.

Families hung stockings by the fire…

And children looked up to the sky wishing for a visit from Santa
Claus before hurrying off to bed…

Meanwhile, Lightning swam into the marina…

A seagull perched high on the mast, saw Lightning's shadow in the

water below and squawked, "Shark! Shark! to alert anyone nearby.

15

Not finding what he was looking for in town…

…Lightning swam out to sea toward a red "star" in the sky.

That star was Rudolph's nose, of course! He and the other reindeer

guided Santa through the night sky, ready to bring toys to good

little girls and boys.

Santa was excited on this crisp, fateful night. With the full moon

shining, he steered his sleigh lower to see his reflection over the

water.

"Just a bit closer", he said to the reindeer.

But Santa leaned too far and fell out of the sleigh down to the cold

waters below!

The reindeer, worried about Santa, crashed in the sea behind him.

They thrashed about in the water and looked nervously at each

other.

Lightning was drawn immediately to all the commotion.

He locked in on the sound. This could be just what he was looking

for.

He circled below Santa and the reindeer…waiting for just the right

moment.

NOW!

Lightning shot up from the deep.

And helped Santa get back up on his sleigh!

Santa was so relieved. He knelt down and gave Lightning a great big hug!

The reindeer breathed a sigh of relief, thanks to their new-found hero.

And Lightning, after years of searching, finally found what he was looking for…

A friend.

Merry Christmas to all.

17153614R00021

Made in the USA
Lexington, KY
21 November 2018